BÊTE NOIRE

FEAR IS JUST A POINT OF VIEW

Editors:

A. W. Gifford
Jennifer L. Gifford

www.betenoiremagazine.com

Bête Noire is published by Dark Opus Press a division of Charm Noir Omnimedia P.O Box 811, Ortonville, MI 48062

ISBN-13: 978-0-9985931-5-9
ISBN-10: 0-9985931-5-X

"All For You, Sara Sue" by Ken Goldman, first appeared in *Night Terrors II* Bloodbound Books (January 2012), *Alone* Thirteen O'Clock Press Horrified Press (April 2016), and *With Candlelight* (e-zine/Online April 15, 2017)

In This Issue

YOU ARE NOT IMMUNE

William Delman

The Bridge Bar was quiet and mostly empty on a Tuesday night. A few townie flies were playing darts back in the corner, while a half-dozen scattered flat screens droned sports highlights.

Jessica had been perched at the bar for an hour, trading glances with a suit sitting alone in a booth. She was finishing off her third beer and languidly swiping at her phone when he finally made his move.

"Hi." He smiled easily, showing off a mouth full of pretty teeth. "My name's Scott. Can I get your next one?" His face was slightly flushed; the friendly tone and casual posture almost masked the hungry, excited look in his eyes. He smelled like agarwood and myrrh.

All in all, she thought her night was looking up.

"Sure, what the hell." She extended her hand. "I'm Jessica. Didn't know people still did this kind of thing."

"What do you mean?" He said, catching the bartender's attention.

"Pick up strangers in bars." She held up her smartphone and made a show of deactivating the dating app she's been perusing through. "You must be pretty old fashioned."

"In some ways." He sat down next to her, flashing his almost too-white teeth again as the bartender brought over a pair of martinis. "I hope you don't mind. I ordered for us."

"Seriously?" She quirked her lips.

"Trust me. I know this doesn't seem like the place for martinis but give it a try."

Jessica took a sip and grinned in surprise. "You're right. This is good." She drained off the rest in one long swallow and set her glass back on the bar. "Hey bartender! Two more."

Scott's face lit up like a screen in the dark. "Uh oh. This looks like trouble." He leaned toward her.

"You have no idea." She winked. "I've got enough troubles to drown this bar."

"Anything I can do to help?"

"We'll see." She laughed and put a hand on his knee.

Scott finished off the rest of his drink as his phone started audibly vibrating in his jacket pocket. He ignored it, keeping his eyes on her, but he pulled back a little.

"Well, I'm glad you liked the martini. I stop here every time I'm in town. I'm in outside sales for a software company."

The bartender returned with their second round and Jessica took another long sip. The alcohol was working like a warm bath on the knots in her neck, even if the booze didn't numb her head like it had in the past.

Scott was still talking. "We do a lot of business with BabelCloud so I'm here for a few days. How about you?"

"Me?" She kneaded his leg with her manicured nails. "I'm bored, and lonely, and you smell good. Maybe you should pay the tab?"

The drive to her hotel took ten minutes, but it had almost been too long. She was pretty sure her underwear was in Scott's car.

"Still want to know what I do for a living?" She said, giving in to an impulse that had building for months. She pushed herself up, leaned back against the headboard, and grabbed the vodka bottle off the nightstand.

"Sure." He yawned.

She took a long pull of the bottle and wiped her mouth with the back of her hand. "Your company, do they offer flu shots?"

"Yeah. Actually, they just made it mandatory this year, unless you get a letter from your doctor."

"I'd get that letter if I were you." Jessica said. "I work for Wellvax. My team travels around the region doing immunization clinics and other stuff for corporate clients. Mostly, they pay for the other stuff. Our 'specialized formulas are designed to improve performance and synergy'."

"Sounds like marketing BS to me."

"Yeah. I'm pretty sure it means we're actually pumping people full of mind-altering nanobots." She took another pull off the bottle.

"You're messing with me." He sat up and motioned for vodka.

"Maybe, but ever since the FDA got privatized things have gotten weird." Jessica took another swig before handing it over. "We're expanding into six countries next year, all developing nations with little to no regulation."

"So, you work for a great company. Are they hiring?" Scott said. Jessica shook her head.

"You don't get it. People come into my cube looking annoyed, worn down, normal. I do my thing, and suddenly wherever we are, it's the greatest place in the universe. They can't wait to get back to work." She shook her head. "It's creepy as hell, watching the change come over people. But it's not the worst part."

"Okay. What's the worst part?"

"Everyone at Wellvax is supposed to be on the shots. They call it a demonstration of brand loyalty. I've only avoided them this long because my boss wants to bang me and he's a bit gullible, so I've been able to string him along."

"Can't go to HR, I guess?"

"And do what, report myself?" Jessica laughed. "I'm telling you, my coworkers are all manically pro-corporate, and fitting in means never forgetting to smile. It's exhausting, but there's no way I'm joining the cult." She rubbed her eyes and snatched the bottle back.

"Why not?" He asked.

She tipped the bottle up and took a swallow. "My mind, my soul, my choice. No employer gets to take me away from me."

"What about your liver?" Scott chuckled.

Jessica shrugged.

"Okay," he said. "Your choice. So why don't you quit?"

"Wellvax pays me three times what I was making before, and I need the money."

"eShopping addiction to maintain?"

"Don't be a dick. My parents got caught in the last housing bubble. I'm helping them stay above water."

"That sucks, about the housing bubble I mean." He said, sounding genuine. "So how long do you think you can hold out?"

"As long as I need to."

"So, you're going to keep smiling and jabbing even though you're miserable and you think you're filling the world with little mind controlling robots, one flu shot at a time?" Scott nodded. "Sorry, but that's a bit nuts. And why are you telling me all this?" His tone wasn't mean, more mildly incredulous and amused, but Jessica still bristled.

"Because, mister judgey, I fake everything with everyone I know, but I don't know you. Be thankful." She sighed. "Anyway, I have to be up early. People to brainwash." She got up and stalked toward the bathroom.

"You're kicking me out?"

"Yup." Jessica shut the door, turned on the shower, and stood there waiting until she finally heard him leave. Then she went back for the vodka.

෴

BabelCloud had stuck them in the gym, privacy cubes and rope queue opposite rows of expensive looking elliptical machines. Her cheery coworkers were clustered by the equipment, loudly admiring the gleaming lines of white plastic and aluminum.

Jessica gave the swarm a wave and her best caffeine fueled smile before walking into her cube. Pulling on a pair of latex gloves, she loaded the first dose into her gun and put some reloads in her pocket.

The employees came in, looking like the usual work-weekend crowd, spirits crushed by endless acronyms. One by one, they signed the electronic waivers and got their shots while the Wellvax app played inspirational montages on the Bluetooth screens behind her.

After the first hour she couldn't look at their faces. Which was why she didn't notice when Scott walked in.

She had just finished reloading the gun when she looked up and saw him, his mouth twitching into a rictus. She noticed he was wearing a wedding band.

Jessica calmly stood, smiled, reached out across the narrow table and leaned in for a kiss. Scott was so surprised he didn't notice the gun until it was pressed against his neck. She pulled the trigger. He grunted and tried to lurch back, but she had a firm grip on his tie.

When he started kissing her back, Jessica pulled away.

"I couldn't let you refuse the shot and run out of here to tell someone why." She said. "I'm sorry."

"For what? It's not like whatever you did erased me memory. I could still walk out of this cube and tell everyone what's happening. Not sure how many people would believe me. Or care." He shrugged. "You knew I would be here today, didn't you?"

"No. I mean, I had a feeling, when you said you did a lot of work with BabelCloud, but—" She trailed off, not sure what else to say. He gave her a disconcertingly sympathetic look and nodded.

"It's always hard to explain."

"What is?" She asked.

"The self-destructive impulse." He held up his hand and pointed to the ring. Then he reached out and gently plucked the gun from her hand.

Her heart was pounding, and her face felt cold. "What's it like?"

"What do you mean?" He found the button along the barrel and pressed it, ejecting the cartridge she'd used on him.

"What do I mean?" She whispered nervously. "What does it feel like, knowing there are a couple million little robots running around inside you right now, rewiring your brain on behalf of your employer?"

"Honestly?" His face was glowing, almost smug. "I'm still not sure I buy that. I've always loved working here, at least I think I have."

As she stood there, he moved past her, plucked a new cartridge from the box on the table, and loaded it into the chamber as though he'd been doing it his whole life.

He turned back toward her. "Here. Let me help you."

"What are you doing?"

He took a step toward her and held up the gun. "One shot. If you're right, the worst thing that can happen is maybe you end up a little happier. And if you're wrong, and you still hate your job and coworkers just as much as before, well at least you won't have to go through your days thinking you are part of some kind of corporate mind-control conspiracy."

She ran through the options in her head.

She could turn around and walk out. She'd probably end up fired. Her parents might lose their house.

Or she could take the shot. Maybe Scott was right, and she was just being paranoid. Or maybe not. But would that really be so bad? She could be a kind of happy, scrubbed free from doubt, and guilt, and herself.

Scott quirked his head. "What do you say?"

She almost made it to her car in the Babelcloud parking garage before her phone started vibrating with texts from her boss.

—Jessica, why did you leave your station?

—Jessica, you can't leave with company property. There are rules. You are not immune!

She was still wearing her lab coat, and she realized there was still a reload in her pocket. A full vial.

—Jessica, please! You can't leave like this.

She reached into her pocket and pulled out the vial. It was small, full of the clear, harmless looking liquid she'd been administering to strangers for nearly two years. For a second, she stood there, one hand clutching the vial, the other holding her key fob, and wondered if she really was being crazy.

Then she heard someone walking up behind her. She turned around in time to watch Scott jab her in the arm with her own gun. He pulled the trigger with a wolfish smile.

"What the hell!" She shoved him back, got in her car, and locked the doors. Then she pulled up her sleeve and checked her arm, just as she started feeling lightheaded.

She realized she was taking rapid, panicked breaths, and Scott was knocking on her window.

"Everything is fine," he said. "Just try to relax."

And she did, because she knew. She was right where she needed to be.

William Delman's *work has previously appeared* in The Arcanist, Little Blue Marble, NewMyths.com, Kzine, The Centropic Oracle, *and many other fine publications. When he's not working on a new story, the best place to find him is on the mats at Fenix Brazilian Jiu-Jitsu in West Peabody, or at home with his family in The Witch City, Salem, Massachusetts. Occasionally, you might also find him on Twitter @DelmanWilliam, or on Facebook* https://www.facebook.com/the2417project

Even Odds

James Dorr

Tickets were sold out
well in advance
for the end of the world,
yet people still lined up—
where else could they go?
The gamblers among us
placed bets on the method,
fire or ice, or another
yet unspecified catastrophe,
but most stood quietly
in ragged ranks,
grateful that God would
have cared enough
to even try.

Indiana short fiction writer and poet James Dorr's The Tears of Isis *was a 2013 Bram Stoker Award® nominee for Superior Achievement in a Fiction Collection. Other books include* Strange Mistresses: Tales of Wonder and Romance, Darker Loves: Tales of Mystery and Regret, *and his all-poetry* Vamps (A Retrospective). *His most recent, out in June 2017 from Elder Signs Press, is a novel-in-stories,* Tombs: A Chronicle of Latter-day Times of Earth. *An Active Member of HWA and SFWA with more than 500 individual appearances from* Alfred Hitchcock's Mystery Magazine *to* Xenophilla, *Dorr invites readers to visit his blog at* http://jamesdorrwriter.wordpress.com.

ANKLE BITER *by Kevin Hurtack*

⊰✠⊱

Kevin Hurtack *works in the traditional medium of pen and ink. He has had a life long fascination with the weird and macabre. You can view more of his work at* kevinhurtack.wordpress.com

A Curse Called Slowness

Abhishek Sengupta

As Kahon jumped from the lighthouse, he remembered he forgot to switch on the night lamp in his daughter's bedroom. She hated darkness, he knew, but darkness loved her.

He hoped his daughter wouldn't wake in the middle of the night. He wished the first streak of sunray that poured in through their windowpane would awaken her. But it was nothing more than wishful thinking.

She would wake in darkness, get down from her bed, hunt for the invisible door and step out of it.

The wind gushed past his face, stung in his eyes, invaded his body through his nose and his mouth. A wetness in its touch. He envisioned his fall to be endless. The distance to the black waters below never wavered.

Kahon had done computations. The height and the force. The angle at which his body would crash into the sea, the water crushing his bones instantly, stopping his heart. His jump was a prolonged contemplation and geometrical precision.

What he hadn't considered, however, was the relativity theory. Time stretching its boundaries; seconds turning into hours; a fraction of a moment mushrooming into a never-ending memory, stretching its tentacles into the night, defiling it with his despair.

Stepping out the invisible door, his daughter would run into the same despair waiting for her outside, smiling at her — a tender look that would also be an invitation. A temptation she won't be able to resist. The despair would turn around, drifting deeper into the misting darkness. She would be following it, a curse called slowness hovering above her head.

"Slow down," Kahon's wife always said, like mothers do, as their daughter ran down the street in the evenings. The little one never paid much heed to her words. Neither her pace nor her giggling sound reverberating in the air, mellowed. The light did – the setting sun, as they returned from the park.

"Let her run," Kahon held his wife's hand, "that's what children do."

"What if she hurts herself?"

"We'll take care, but that shouldn't stop her from being a child." He pressed her palm, "We're always there behind her, aren't we?"

The spot he had jumped from lay behind him now.

Did he regret having left it behind?

The spot.

That's all it ever was.

The place he would hit the sea was a spot too.

How were the two different from each other?

After the accident, the place where they discovered his wife's body had been a spot as well. Doctors defined her death with the same term.

Spot dead.

He went visiting the accident spot later. It looked like any other spot.

How was it powerful enough to take his wife away in a flash and ruthless enough to leave an even darker spot in the mind of their little one?

Her daughter hated that darkness ever since. She preferred the night lamp to be on when she slept. On nights he would forget to keep it on, she rose in the middle of the night and walked out her room, outside the house. She followed a solitary despair in the dark; sauntering, stumbled right onto the beach, stepped into the broken waves playing down the shore, and stopped. Stopping was the most frightening part for her; it revived her conscious self. Darkness enveloping her, she stood at a spot where the sea began. The same spot every night, until she traced her way back home, all alone.

"I dreamt of mum," she said in the mornings, still weeping.

Kahon held her in her arms. "We'll be fine."

He'd still be fine, he knew, as gravity made him its plaything. A fall changes nothing. Nor a death. Not his. The endless sea waited for him, to cradle him in its arms, hiding him away from the repetitive slowness.

For him, slowness started when his daughter stopped running down the streets, spiralling further as a weariness grabbed hold of her. Tiresome eyes followed by tiring feet until her entire body grew tired. Slowness got infused in everything she did, even into things she didn't do and merely thought of. She needed time to think. To breathe. The nights further deepened her curse.

Despite her weariness, she would still walk out into the night in the exact inopportune moment Kahon fell asleep even after his sincerest efforts to stay vigilant.

His sincerest efforts.

Never enough.

She became much too exhausted. Too weary to breathe even. The physicians and their prescriptions failed, so they ended up writing a certificate for her, mentioning her time of death.

Did that really happen?

Still every night, Kahon could hear the sound of her bedroom door creaking and then, the main door. Still every night, he needed to keep her night lamp on to save her from the despair in the dark.

But he forgot to turn it on that night when he came to take the final plunge. Falling, Kahon imagined his daughter walking towards the shore, the curse called slowness still hovering above her head.

The sea in front of him disappeared into a dark as his eyes turned hazy. Shadows appeared it its place. Shadows, like smog, flew ahead of him – as if he were chasing them. Something melancholy in the way the shadows fell. Something slow. It reminded him of the despair in the dark his daughter often mentioned following. Her mother.

Is that you? He asked, although never uttering.

The shadows didn't respond, taking him down like a silent guide, languid in its movement.

For the first time, he understood slowness. It completed his fall. Made it eternal. Unending.

Or perhaps, it had already ended.

It didn't matter anymore.

He pictured his daughter stepping into the water tonight but never stopping—until they met where the sea turned slow.

Abhishek Sengupta *is imaginary. Mostly, people would want to believe that he writes fiction & poetry which borders on Surrealism and Magical Realism, and is stuck inside a window in Kolkata, India, but he knows none of it is true. He doesn't exist. Only his imaginary writing does, and have appeared or are forthcoming in* Flapperhouse, Outlook Springs, Liminality, Thrice Fiction, *and others. According to a rumour doing its rounds, he is also known to be adding final touches to his magical realism novel, but it may be nothing more than a myth. If you're gifted, however, you may also imagine him in Twitter* **@AbhishekSWrites** *or in his hypothetical website -* www.abhishek-sengupta.com

Elemental Gnomes

Bruce Boston

Far beneath the crust of Earth,
beyond the mantle, within its bowels,
in burrowed caves and tunnels

dimly lighted by an edible fungus,
a race of Elementals thrives.
Gnomes by name, hunched,

pale diminutive creatures,
their language only grunts
and gestures, their hands

and fingers and teeth so strong
they cannot only dig through
hard-packed dirt but solid rock.

They take their mates for life
and realize their desires in
dark side tunnels stripped

of the luminescent fungus.
There they find a sleep
like death until it is time

to start digging again.
As their new tunnels grow,
the old collapse behind.

Gravity claims its own
in broken passages.
There is no going back.

When the last of their kind
vanish from the bowels
of the Earth, when the last

of their tunnels collapse,
there will be nothing
left of them whatsoever.

Bruce Boston *is the author of more than fifty books and chapbooks, includ-ing the dystopian sf novel* The Guardener's Tale *and the psychedelic com-ing-of-age-novel* Stained Glass Rain. *His poems and/or fiction have ap-peared in* Asimov's SF, Analog, Weird Tales, Amazing, Daily Science Fiction, *the* Nebula Awards Anthology *and* Year's Best Fantasy and Horror. *His poetry has received the* Bram Stoker Award, *the* Asimov's Readers Award, *the* Balticon Poetry Award, *and the* Rhysling *and* Grandmaster Awards *of the SFPA. His fiction has received a* Pushcart Prize, *and twice been a finalist for the* Bram Stoker Award *(novel, short story).* www.bruceboston.com

SEVEN

Pauline Yates

It's my forty-ninth birthday and today one of my well-wishers will die. A death has occurred every seventh year since the day I kicked my foot through the wall of my mother's uterus. My father didn't blame me for her death. It was a difficult birth, he said. But he stopped wishing me a happy birthday when, on my twenty-first, his golfing buddy dropped by to wish me well and then choked to death on a plastic flower that decorated my cake.

I didn't understand why my father stopped with the birthday wishes until I turned twenty-eight. I was in the maternity ward giving birth to the first of my three daughters. Unlike my own mother's, the birthing was easy. My daughter arrived five minutes before midnight, the day before my birthday. When I woke in the morning, my room was filled with flowers and cards from family and friends. My father was the first to arrive, but he grew nervous when my tending nurse wished me a happy birthday. As she rearranged the flowers, she was stung by a bee. Her throat swelled to the size of a football. Despite being rushed to the emergency room, she died from anaphylactic shock twenty minutes later.

That's when my father sat down and told me the truth about my previous seventh year birthdays. My little friend Jane didn't move to another country. She never recovered from the hit on the head as we smashed the piñata at my seventh birthday party. And on my fourteenth birthday, the cute boy who sneaked a birthday kiss didn't die from meningitis. He cut his foot on the way home and bled to death in his sleep. My father didn't know why I was cursed with the seven-year death, nor could he explain the random pattern of who dies. Perhaps I inherited it from my mother, he said. She never could own a cat that lived past the age of seven.

The sadness in my father's eyes remained with me through my thirty-fifth and forty-second birthdays. On those days, I stayed indoors and hid beneath the bed sheets, refusing to acknowledge my special day. It didn't make any difference. The postman called out best wishes as he delivered a birthday card to the letterbox. He was dead two minutes later from a heart attack. And although I'd set my birthday to private on my Facebook page, an old friend remembered and posted a happy birthday message on my timeline. I heard she tripped and fell into her children's wading pool. She drowned in twelve inches of water.

Since I cannot avoid this seven-year death, I plan to speed up the process so I can get on with enjoying my day. I'm having a party. My husband is thrilled since I've never been keen to celebrate. My three daughters took care of all the planning. My only insistence was we hold the party at the local hall, which is big enough to hold the number of guests I've invited. What I don't tell my family is I don't want the job of cleaning blood off the carpet should death show its face inside our house.

My daughters did a fabulous job on the decorating. The old timber hall is decked out with streamers and balloons. Candles float in punch bowls. Platters of finger food adorn the tables. My birthday cake sits in the middle, a caramel-filled sponge complete with forty-nine candles. I stuck a chewy toffee in the icing. My grandfather is stricken with terminal cancer. Maybe the toffee will get stuck in his dentures and he'll choke.

The first guests arrive at seven. I cast my eye over aunts and uncles I barely know and friends I haven't seen in years. I make a special point of kissing their partners. I'll feel better if death snatches someone I'm not well acquainted with. When my father arrives, he stays to the side of the hall. My husband notices his aloofness. When he asks why my dad bothered to come if he can't take a moment to wish me a happy birthday, I laugh and say it's a private joke between me and my dad.

The party is a success, but not so for tempting death. I thought I'd covered all bases. I filled bowls with peanuts to cause allergic reactions. I gave bags of marbles to the children to roll across the dance floor. At the top of the back steps, I removed a light bulb and spilled a glass of water so the top step is slippery. But despite my efforts, the only emergency needing attention was when a cousin slit his finger on the shard of glass I hid in the ice cube bucket. All he needed was a band-aid.

At ten minutes to twelve, I panic. Somebody has to die, but the last guest has left and all who remain are my father and my family. My father retreats to a corner of the hall and sits down with his arms crossed. My husband, drunk on his feet, joins him. Terrified for my daughters, I tell them to stay exactly where they are for the next ten minutes. They roll their eyes as though age has addled my brain and start to clean up. I follow their every move, but when my youngest climbs on a chair and starts to pull down the party streamers, I freak out. I scream at her to get off the chair before she falls but all I do is attract the attention of my husband. He staggers towards me, a goofy grin on his face. Then he starts to sing me a happy birthday. I manage to clamp my hand over his mouth before he says, 'to you', but he's so drunk he breaks into a fit of laughter. And then he has a choking fit. Horrified, I smack him on the back and plead with death not to take my husband. But his face turns a deadly shade of blue.

There's nothing I can do. No amount of screaming, or pleading, or selling my soul will save my husband from this birthday death wish. In the last minute to midnight, my father strides across the room, grabs my shoulders and spins me around so we stand face to face. He gives me smile that only a father can give a daughter then kisses my cheek and whispers, "Happy birthday, Susa—"

He drops dead at my feet. He didn't even get to finish my name. The coroner listed brain aneurysm as the cause of death, but if my father had his way, I'm sure he'd amend the report to read 'Sacrifice'. As for my husband, the shock of seeing my father die stopped his choking attack. I'm not going to tell him the truth. Some things are best left buried.

Pauline Yates *writes everything from historical fiction to hard sci-fi, but her weakness is for comedy, which likes to sneak into her work. More of her stories can be found at* Metaphorosis, Abyss and Apex, The Casket of Fictional Delights, *and* Every Day Fiction. *She is the author of* Rumours Uncut, *a digital interactive thriller for Story City, and is a contributing author to the* 5x5 Reading and Score *anthologies published by Metaphorosis Books. Pauline lives in Australia. Follow her on Twitter @midnightmuser1.*

POEM FOR THE LAST VICTIM

John Grey

It takes more than just the dark.
Someone even darker is required.
I could explain why
the sun disappears over the horizon
in a few short sentences
but the complications and contradictions
of the human psyche
are unfathomable.
So if the creaking sound can be explained,
this is not really night.
Same as if the window rattle
is from a high-powered breeze.
Night is nothing without the threat.
It's just day with the lights out
if you don't share it
with a forbidding stranger.
No, night's not night
unless there's someone standing
in the bedroom doorway.
And, even then,
it's not night for long.

John Grey *is an Australian poet, US resident. Recently published in* Front Range Review, Studio One *and* Columbia Review *with work upcoming in* Naugatuck River Review, Abyss and Apex *and* Midwest Quarterly.

ALL FOR YOU, SARA SUE

Ken Goldman

The moment a child is born,
the mother is also born.
She never existed before.
The woman existed, but the mother, never.
A mother is something absolutely new.

- Bhagwan Shree Rajneesh (1931-1990)

Would it mean anything now if I told you that I loved my husband? I know that's hard for you to swallow considering what's happened, but I do mean it. No woman could ask for a finer man than my Elliot, least of all a woman like myself. Just look at the sacrifices he made for us. How could anyone with a beating heart not love a man who would suffer for his loved ones like that? And we did love our Sara Sue so much, you know, so very much.

Ever notice how in those Hollywood movies these beautiful couples always manage to meet real cute? Some Jennifer Aniston type breaks her heel on the streets of New York and then — *Wham!* This prince of a guy shows up to help her, he just materializes out of thin air for lovely Jennifer, and he's usually some beef cake, or maybe he has this really charming accent every woman in the audience immediately goes wet for. And of course, despite the inevitable complications, love happens in the space of the next ninety minutes, during which time for the women in the theater there's not a dry seat in the house. Everything wraps so perfectly, just in time to cue the syrupy love song they run with the end credits. Yeah, those movies, they're always the same. Some boy wins some girl, but then loses said girl or she loses him, and then—well, I've already told you the rest. My point is, everyone goes home happy.

I'd like to say that's how it happened with Elliot and me. Yes, I'd like to, but I can't. Oh, we started happy enough during one rainy afternoon when he sat alongside me at the Charlestown Avenue Starbucks and didn't speak a word for ten minutes. See, it was crowded, and that seat was the only one available. And when he finally did speak, he asked me for the time. I gave it to him, he thanked me, and—well, end of story. Almost. Because when I ran into him on the bus later that day, again only one seat was available. So, I sat next to him expecting at most a smile of recognition. But no, that man spoke right up.

"Well, this must be kismet," that's what he said, and only then did I realize how attractive he was. Not movie star attractive, of course, but easy enough on the eyes. I'll admit I was startled the man said anything considering I sat there soaking wet and looked awful. I mean, look at me. Do I have the kind of face men would remember?

"What's that?" I asked.

"Kismet. From this old late show '50's musical of the same name. It means fate, destiny. And I'd say there must be some kind of fate working here, sitting next to each other again like this, wouldn't you?" He smiled, offered his hand. "My name is Elliot. And who might your soaking wet self be?"

I smiled but didn't answer his question. The man seemed to be coming on to me, and that didn't happen often—or ever. So instead I said the first thing that came to mind, which was unfortunately something stupid.

"Elliot. That was my father's name. He's dead now."

Dumb, I know. But my hesitation didn't put that man off for one second. "It's not a name you can do much with. Too humdrum to shorten into anything. Not much wiggle room to do that. I mean, come on—El? Ellie? Try surviving the school yard when kids call you that."

I smiled politely again, although I could feel my heart beginning to race. We seemed pretty awkward talking such nonsense, so I went for the save, leaning closer as if sharing a secret. It was a daring move for me. "My real name is Darcella Etheridge, but everyone calls me Darcy. I'm not sure how that started, but I'm glad it did. Anyway, you can call me anything you like." I had no idea what that meant, but Elliot seemed to think I had said something very clever. He grinned, leaned close too.

"So, you're suggesting I call you?"

It wasn't the stuff great romance stories are made of, I know. But that's how we began, and by the end of our bus ride I felt I had been talking with an old friend. No Reese or Julia or Jennifer meeting Hugh Jackman or Clive whats-his-name while Celine Dion warbles on the soundtrack. Attractive as Elliot appeared, I doubt anyone would mistake him for Mr. Jackman, or me for — well, I can name about a hundred movie stars to whom I bear no resemblance whatsoever. But to Mr. Elliot Hanover, that didn't matter in the least. And when he spoke my name my heart pretty much supplied its own soundtrack. I suppose I'm getting much too talky about that first day, so I'll go easy on all the love stuff that followed. Oh yes, there was quite a bit of that, in case you were wondering, but I'll skip to the serious parts you ought to know about, okay?

We married. It didn't take long. A woman knows when it feels right. Hell, I practically jumped into that man's arms when he asked me to be his. Somehow, he managed to present me with a beautiful ring too, although to this day I couldn't tell you how he could afford such a thing working in the city mail room at the time. But we were both so young, and with youth comes foolishness. I've no doubt Elliot probably spent most of his life savings on what he placed on my finger.

Our wedding ceremony wasn't anything to make those English Royals envious and the small apartment we moved into fell considerably short of palatial, but none of that mattered. I knew this was as perfect a life as I'd ever hoped for, and only one thing could make it more perfect. Elliot felt the same, so we got to working on beginning our family right away. We were young. We didn't know — we just didn't know. See, it wasn't really anyone's fault, my not being able to conceive, but it didn't seem in the stars for us. So after many months trying, we decided to find out if maybe we had been doing something wrong. Turns out it wasn't Elliot or me who got it wrong. No, nature herself had made that decision for us; it was what Elliot had called kismet. Well, fate can kismet my ass. Dr. Byron over at the County Medical Hospital, he informed us that my eggs weren't doing what a woman's eggs are supposed to. But that wasn't all. Because, see, Dr. Byron also tested Elliot, and — well, let's just say that Mother Nature decided to hit us with a double barrel. I must have cried myself to sleep for weeks.

"We can adopt," Elliot tried reassuring me. "I swear, we would love that child like it was our own, Darcy, I'm sure we would." But I knew it wouldn't be the same, not for me, and besides, we could never afford what those agencies were asking. Talk about a hard pill to swallow, and I really did try. But knowing that I could never be a mother, that I could never hold my own infant in my arms, it was just too much for me to stand.

That's how Sara Sue came to be. She was Elliot's idea, and maybe at first, I thought it seemed crazy. After I'd spent so many nights bathing my face in tears, one morning Elliot sat on the bed alongside me. He wore this huge grin, something I hadn't seen for weeks. Taking my face into his hands, he kissed me.

"I think maybe we're going to have that child after all. See, I've been doing some thinking, Darcy, and I believe you're going to give birth to our child any day now."

I had no idea what he meant. Unless my new husband intended to kidnap some infant from its crib, I didn't see any child in our future. But doing something so wrong wasn't Elliot Hanover's style. I sat up, managed a few words.

"You want to tell me how that's going to happen, considering the doctor explained that a newborn coming out of me is as likely as one coming out of that old bowling ball of yours?"

Elliot's grin grew wider. He rubbed my stomach, then put his ear to it. "Why, I believe I've just felt that baby of ours kick. She's going to be a healthy one, our Sara Sue, I just know it. I'm so proud of you, Darcy. You'll be be such a wonderful mother." He turned serious. "Are you following me on this?"

"Not at all." I'll tell you right now that at that moment I felt certain my Elliot had completely lost his mind. Either that, or he had something up his sleeve I couldn't begin to guess. As it turned out, he did.

"Okay, then, I'll explain this only once, and after today I'll never say another word about it. You can either agree to it or not. Whatever you decide will be all right, but I'm hoping you'll see this situation the way I do."

I might have felt frightened had those words come from a man less rational than my husband, but I knew he was dead serious and that his feelings for me never had proved less than solid gold genuine.

Elliot took my hand, held it tight. His words sounded as if he had rehearsed them for hours. Likely, he had. But he spoke with such assuredness, such certainty...

"Our Sara Sue will be born in a few days. We'll need time to fix up the place, of course, maybe purchase an old crib at the thrift store, some baby clothes too. You'll deliver a little prematurely at home, and it may seem somewhat touch and go for a while, but I'll be there to deliver our child and it will be a perfect birth. And from that day forward you and I, together we'll watch our daughter grow every day, and we'll ask her how her time at school went, soothe her when she skins her knee, laugh and cry with her when circumstances call for it. Most important, we'll love that little girl every bit as much as if—"

He seemed to almost choke on the rest of that sentence. I finished it for him.

"As if she were real?"

Those words did not come easy. I looked hard into my husband's eyes to determine if maybe something had gone seriously wrong with his thinking to cause him to suggest something so preposterous. But I saw a clarity there that I knew meant he had earnestly weighed the pros and cons of his proposition.

"She *will* be real, Darcy. To us she'll be more real than anything else in the world."

Elliot squeezed my hand, then kissed it. "Our Sara Sue will be the most perfect child a parent could want, and you—*you* will be the perfect mother."

I didn't know whether to laugh or cry. I did neither. What Elliot had suggested was possibly the most insane idea a man could propose, or maybe it was the most incredible demonstration of love of which any husband was capable. Knowing my man the way I did, I didn't have to question his reasoning for very long.

"Why Sara Sue?" I asked.

His smile reappeared. "You wanted a girl, right?"

I nodded.

"Well, then, why *not* Sara Sue?"

Thinking over what he suggested, I felt so much love for my husband I knew no other response would do. Elliot had found a way to give us our child, and I threw my arms around him, held him as close as I could. "I know our Sara Sue will be perfect," I whispered. "I know she will."

It was an amazing moment, all right. I was laughing while tears clouded my eyes. And Elliot and I, we held each other so tight for the next hour as if we were each afraid to let go.

And maybe we were.

Elliot proved true to his word. Never once did he imply that Sara Sue would be anything less than our flesh and blood daughter. So, I played along, even down to his providing all the skills necessary to make our imaginary child's imaginary birth anything but imaginary. I'll spare you the details of that day, but I will admit that I screamed and pushed just as accurately as any woman going through the wonderful agony of childbirth, and Elliott stood by me the whole time wiping my forehead with a moist towel while coaxing my breathing. When it was over, I felt exhausted, and I really was bathed in sweat. Moments later, there stood Elliot holding the most beautiful imaginary infant a new mother could ever hope to see. Yes, I knew that wrapped inside the pink blanket was probably a bag of flour, but I swear, for a moment I really did see our new daughter in her father's arms. And I'm telling no lie when I say my heart nearly burst with happiness when he handed Sara Sue to me.

In the days that followed when Elliott returned from work his first words always were "Where's my little angel? What wonderful thing did our daughter do today?" And I would answer, I'd say "Oh, you should have seen her! She was so good, Elliot, the way she ate all her carrots, and without so much as a whimper the entire afternoon. She's fast asleep now. Come, look." But sometimes Sara Sue could be difficult too, and I'd complain, "Oh, God! I think I want to scream. That child just refused to eat anything today, and I must have changed her diaper ten times!"

During the night Elliot often would climb from our bed, tell me "I hear Sara Sue crying. You go back to sleep, Darcy. I'll take care of it." Other times I would sit for an hour rocking her to sleep and singing gently to her "Hush little baby, don't say a word ..."

And so it went ...

"Oh, Elliot! Sara Sue spoke her first word today! Mama — she said Mama!!"

"Look, Darcy! I think — Yes! I think she's trying to take her first step right now!"

"Hush little baby ..."
"Who's Daddy's perfect little angel? Who? Who?"
"First day of school! Let's get going, munchkin!"
"Elliot, come see what our daughter drew in class today!"
"Love you ... Love you ..."

No there was nothing there to see, I knew that. But another part of me disregarded that empty space, and instead I saw the most precious girl child on this planet. And like a madly spinning carousel the years seemed to pass too quickly...

"Sara Sue got picked for head cheerleader today, Elliot. Head cheerleader!"
"Doesn't our daughter look beautiful all dressed up for the dance?"
"Tell her, Elliot. Tell her how boys sometimes can seem cruel like that ..."

Sara Sue came laughing to us when she saw the first robin of spring, told how she caught lightning bugs inside a jar on the first day of summer, rolled in the autumn leaves or made snow angels in the park. They were such wonderful years. Sara Sue was our life.

No, that's not correct. She was more.

Sara Sue kept us alive!

But then during the darkest days of winter our old friend Kismet reared her ugly head. Elliot came from our daughter's room. "Darcy, do Sara Sue's eyes look a bit swollen to you? She's been complaining about stomach pains and she can't seem to move. I think there's something seriously wrong."

Of course, I realized a child's illness was a problem all parents face. Our daughter was an adolescent now but never had she been sick, so some kind of illness seemed inevitable. I entered Sara Sue's room, looked into the empty bed and waited a respectable few minutes. Returning to my husband I told him "You may be right, she doesn't look so good. There's some fever too." Then I added the only thing a concerned parent would say. "I think maybe we should see the doctor."

I had barely got that sentence out before Elliot grabbed his coat, so I went for mine. But he told me, "No, Darcy, you stay home," always wanting to protect me from anything disturbing. Although my maternal instincts disagreed, I chose not to argue, certain that within the hour Elliot would return, explain to me that our daughter had just caught a bad virus, or something like that. I heard him tell Sara Sue to put on some clothes, watched through the window as our old Camry drove off.

For hours I waited but Elliot didn't return, and when I called his cellular he didn't answer. I prayed our Sara Sue would be all right, all the while realizing the foolishness of that prayer. I suppose when you believe in something hard enough, you make it so. That night I realized how authentic Sara Sue had become to both of us, understood the fear any mother would feel for her ailing child. Near dawn Elliot appeared at the door. I could tell he hadn't slept, and the look on his face was one I had never seen.

"Sara Sue isn't with you?" I asked.

Without removing his coat, he sat on the couch, just looked at me. "Darcy, I think you had better sit too." Taking his hand, I could feel his trembling. "It was her heart, Darcy. The doctors, they tried and tried, but Sara Sue just wasn't strong enough. She didn't make it."

The world stopped in that instant, and I couldn't form even the simplest rational thought. "That's—That's not possible, Elliot. She's just a young girl, hardly into her teenage years. A child's heart—*our* child's, it just doesn't quit like that. It *can't!*"

"Sara Sue's heart did. It just stopped, Darcy, like some busted watch. Just like that."

[She isn't real, Elliot. She never was. You know it. I know it. How can she die?]

But Elliot insisted our child lay in the morgue at County Medical. I heard growing anger in his voice, and I reached for him, but he pulled himself from me, told me he needed to be alone for a while. I understood, or at least a part of me thought I did. I'm certain we never felt so lonely in our lives as we mourned the tragic death of our child, arranged for her burial, spoke of her funeral—all without leaving our apartment. We opened imaginary cards of sympathy from imaginary friends, shared them, answered imaginary calls. I guess after all those years I just got caught up in the pretending, and I almost believed our daughter's death to be so. I knew Sara Sue seemed real—*but she wasn't!* Still, the grief felt as real as anything I'd experienced, although what followed after weeks of mourning our loss—well, I couldn't have seen it coming in a million years.

Searching for answers, at first, I believed maybe Elliot decided Sara Sue had to die because he hoped we might grow closer in our grief. But that didn't happen. We stopped talking, ate little, slept less.

Sometimes Elliot disappeared for the entire night. I knew better than to ask where he had been because the alcohol on his breath told me. But that wasn't the worst of it. Often at night Elliot would leave our bed and scream like a man gone mad. I could no longer suggest that our Sara Sue existed only in our imaginations. He would glare at me as if I had uttered something reprehensible, my words deserving no response beyond his complete contempt that I had suggested such a terrible thing. His misery grew so terrible that now it seemed I mourned more for my lost husband than for Sara Sue.

I should have seen it coming — I should have seen it!

He had managed to do it so quietly while I slept, I never heard a sound from the bathroom. I found Elliot in the morning slumped in a spreading puddle of his own blood, the razor's blade still in his wrist, a smeared note at his side.

> I'm so sorry, Darcy. I just can't take the pain any more.
>
> I love you.

I won't go into the details of the awful scene I found. I really can't do that without bringing myself back to it. Seeing my beloved husband there on the floor, and the blood, so much blood — well, just talking about it, I'm sorry, but I don't want to say any more about that. I can't tell you how I felt either. I couldn't get my mind to comprehend what Elliot had done or why he had done it. I still can't. No matter how I look at it, it makes no sense at all. Well, maybe that's not entirely true. See, I always knew my Elliot was more man than a woman like me ever deserved, and I love him still despite the terrible thing he did. So, there's one thing I do understand. It's been almost a year now since my husband and our Sara Sue have been gone, and that one thing rings pretty clear.

Loneliness, it does terrible things to a person's head — terrible things.

Yes, I know it wasn't right, my taking that infant from its carriage. But when I saw her at the Charlestown Mall left unattended for that moment — well, I just did what I did without putting much thought into it. That little darling looked so much like our Sara Sue, it seemed my hands developed a mind of their own when they snatched her. After I'd done that, all I could think to do was just run. So, there I was, standing in the middle of that parking lot holding some strange woman's infant, having not the slightest idea what to do next. I found this large plastic trash bag in a bin, emptied it to put the infant inside. I wanted to hide her, that was all. I wasn't thinking clearly, you have to know that. I just wasn't thinking clearly.

Would it mean anything now if I told you how sorry I feel for all I've done? Because I do feel sorry, you know — so very sorry for whatever sorrow I've caused. It's just that I miss my family so much, even knowing our Sara Sue never really — she never —

...not really...

Damn! Oh damn!

Do you think you could turn off that recorder device now, please, Sergeant? I've told you all there is to tell, and I'm feeling so tired.

5th POLICE PRECINCT : CITY OF CHARLESTOWN
12: 47 a.m.

After a third replay of the recorded confession of the woman who called herself Mrs. Darcella Hanover, Sergeant Harry Servitto felt damned tired himself. Arresting officer Will McCormack poured two cups of coffee and spoke Harry's thoughts.

"She's wrong about that last part, Sergeant. There's more to tell, all right. A dozen witnesses saw her take that child, a dozen more claim there always seemed something not right about her. I saw that close up when we busted that woman's door and found her singing some 'Hush Little Baby' song to that stolen infant's corpse. Never looked up, just kept singing her damned lullaby like we weren't there, as if that dead baby was gurgling happily in her own mother's arms."

Servitto raised a pair of bloodshot eyes. "To that woman you *weren't* there, William. People see what they want to see. Maybe doing that, they goose up fate into being whatever they want it to be. She wanted a real Sara Sue. I guess she found one. But fate has her way of biting you in the ass. Kismet, like the lady said." He stubbed out his cigarette, stared at the ashes. "Christ, it's too late to be getting philosophical."

Looking as tired as his superior, McCormack sipped his coffee. "Go figure what crazy shit goes on inside a lonely woman's head to make her self-destruct like that, eh? Guess we'll have to let the court shrink decide that."

Servitto nodded agreement. "You find anything about this Hanover guy?"

The officer shook his head. "Not a damned thing, Sergeant. Elliot's her late father's name, Hanover's the family name of some local garage mechanic says he took this Darcella to a movie once when she was about fifteen, and he hasn't seen her since. But there's no record of any Elliot Hanover in this woman's life, not a signature on any document or canceled check, not one person in that apartment building who's ever seen a trace of the man. No one's never seen her sporting any fancy ring like she spoke about, neither. She's never been anything but Darcella Etheridge. Court shrink's going to have a field day with this one."

Servitto forced a tired smile, quickly gave it up and reached for his coffee.

"Loneliness is one mean mind fucker, all right. A woman wants a family, she figures a way to have one. Imaginary dead children and husbands don't mean a whole lot, legally speaking. But now we've got a dead infant for real here. Write it up by tomorrow morning, will you? Go home and kiss your wife and kids." He glared into his cup. "Anything else, William?"

The young officer took a moment to consider the question. He shrugged.

"Coffee's gone cold," he said.

Ken Goldman, *former Philadelphia teacher of English and Film Studies, is an affiliate member of the Horror Writers Association. He has homes on the Main Line in Pennsylvania and at the Jersey shore. His stories have appeared in over 900 independent press publications in the U.S., Canada, the UK, and Australia with over twenty due for publication in 2019. Since 1993 Ken's tales have received seven honorable mentions in* The Year's Best Fantasy & Horror. *He has written five books: three anthologies of short stories,* You Had Me At ARRGH!! *(Sam's Dot Publishers),* Donny Doesn't Live Hear Anymore *(A/A Productions) and* Starcrossed *(Vampires 2); and a novella,* Desiree, *(Damnation Books). His first novel,* Of a Feather *(Horrific Tales Publishing) was released in January 2014.* Sinkhole, *his second novel, was published by Bloodshot Books August 2017.*

Marge Simon

"Give me a head with hair, long beautiful hair
Shining, gleaming, streaming, flaxen, waxen
Give me down to there, hair, shoulder length or longer
Here baby, there, momma, everywhere, daddy, daddy…"
"I want long, straight, curly, fuzzy, snaggy, shaggy, ratty, matty
Oily, greasy, fleecy, shining, gleaming, streaming, flaxen, waxen …" *
and bloody —

that's the part she had a problem with, at first,
but she learned to let the scalp pieces
dry out by putting them
under her big sister's tanning lamp.

Oh, yes, that worked well.
A bit of airplane glue affixed the swatch;
the snaggy, shaggy, ratty, matty
tangled, spangled and spaghettied
tufts didn't all match up on her dolly,
but the result was splendid, all the same.

The real problem she now faced was
disposing of the remains of her little girlfriends.

*lyrics excerpted from the long-running musical, "HAIR".

⊂⊰⧲⊱⊃

Marge Simon lives in Ocala, FL. She edits a column for the HWA Newsletter, "Blood & Spades: Poets of the Dark Side," *and serves on Board of Trustees. She is the second woman to be acknowledged by the SF &F Association with a Grand Master Award. She has won* the Bram Stoker Award, the Rhysling Award, Elgin, Dwarf Stars and Strange Horizons Readers' Award. *Marge's poems and stories have appeared in* Silver Blade, Bête Noire, Urban Fantasist, Daily Science Fiction *and serves on the board of the Speculative Literary Foundation.* www.margesimon.com

KILLER

Alice Andersen

He had the look of an assassin about him — dark bulging eyes set inside a round, bulbous head, a solid fellow, not afraid to look me in the eye. As I turned to walk away, his silence drew me back to the cage where I re-read the tag. "Elliot T. Carnage, nickname 'Killer', Chihuahua, 4 years old, non-aggressive, well-trained, owner deceased."

The humane society covered the basic details of the abandoned dog and left my imagination to fill in the blanks. A blue-clad employee walked by, immune to the howls of loneliness following her path down the rows of cages. "Excuse me," I said to stop her, "do you know how this dog got his nickname?"

She looked down at the petite pup that cocked his ears and looked up, as if waiting to hear the story for himself. "You don't want that dog." She wagged her finger in his direction. "He killed his owner."

"What!" I couldn't believe what I'd just heard.

"I'm not making it up. The granddaughter saw the whole thing. Killer ran right in front of the old lady and tripped her as she headed down the stairs. He earned his nickname."

I checked out the other dogs at the pound, wanting a domineering, aggressive animal for protection, but adopted the sweet little Chihuahua in the end. Killer would make the perfect gift for my abusive, drunken SOB husband. I held the tiny, innocent creature with love as I planned out his training sessions.

Alice Andersen *lives in the Rocky Mountains with a math teacher. To escape from quadratic equations, she hides out on her computer writing mystery, romance, and fantasy novels with quirky characters and plenty of action. When not working on a novel, she writes flash fiction and short stories with sometimes diabolical and sometimes humorous endings. Alice is a member of RMFW and RWA. She has a degree in writing from Colorado Mesa University. Although living in Colorado, she grew up on the gulf coast and remains a Texan at heart.*

Bill Thomas *is a cartoonist who founded a cartoon and graphic business with his brother Bob called Thomastoons. Bill went to college for graphics and has had his work appear in numerous magazines. He loves crafting humor and takes great joy in making people laugh or smile. So make his day.*

What Happens to Would-Be Refugees

Ronald A. Busse

High tide marches in its steady cadence as
she stands on the shore open-mouthed, stupefied.
Saturated sea air weighs down her long, anchor-chain
hair braids, sloshing in lather — thick and
polluted — that shampoos the shore.

Eyes wide to a fog-filled lavender sky lit by
moonbeams, she finally finds her voice and beckons,
"Come back! Don't leave me here with them!"
But her words seem to die before they can reach
her long-gone deserters.

A slanted crescent-moon slips her a sly smile.
She squints back a look of disgust, when — are those
rotten teeth she sees in its mouth-hole? — a towering
wave unleashes its fury over her head,
briefly cutting off her air supply.

As the water recedes, she looks down
and gasps,
tries to move her legs…
can't.
Sandy muck entombs her thigh high.
She wonders,

"How long have I been standing here since the takeover?"

Another wave — bigger.
She holds her breath… holds…
exhales…
gulps in rancid sea air
in harsh gasps.

A faded-blue plastic bucket — its white plastic handle
half-dislodged, dangling from one side —
washes back and forth just out of reach,
out and in.

Her too big eyes bore a tunnel upward,
locking with an unfeeling crescent that laughs harder,
foul teeth seem bigger,
its impact craters deep and dark and throbbing,
as if they were having root canals.

Arms still free, she could grab that bucket
and dig herself out!
But it continues its in-and-out journey
to nowhere —
near reach but nearing no closer,
as if to taunt her.

Lavender moonbeams deepen to violaceous lasers,
liquefying the velvet fog. Her arms lift
involuntarily above her head,
anchor-chain braids stand at attention,
legs loosen from wet sand with a lifting sensation
as the moon exerts all of its gravitational pull.
A tidal wave swells.

Earth counters,
flexes its magnetic muscles,
yanking her back down —
down through the hole she made in the sand,
down past layers of putty-colored muck,
down through its viscous asthenosphere;

her last feeling that
of molten mantle
sliding
up her
naked body.

Pitchforks poke at the ceiling in anticipation.

Ronald A. Busse's *poetry has appeared in* Star*Line, FreeXpresSion, The Poet's Art, *and* The Poet's Corner. *He's also self-published a poetry book titled* Into the Retrospectrum *and is currently writing his second book.*

There's Something in the Water

Luke Chapman

There's something in the water," the little girl said taking a bite out of a chocolate chip ice cream cone.

"What do you mean there's something in the water?" Benny replied.

"I mean," she exaggerated, "I saw something move under the water." Her legs kicked back and forth over the stony edge.

"Uh-huh, sure there is."

"You'll see, just wait. It'll show up again," she said taking a neat lick off the cone.

The winds of the earlier thunderstorm blew across the inky man-made lake causing dark ripples to slide across the glass surface. It had been weeks since the humidity wasn't thick as snot and the breeze felt wonderful. The surrounding mist from the lakes many fountains cooled his hot skin. He took a deep breath, filling his head with the Earthy smell of wet grass and fresh rain.

It's finally over Benny-boy, he thought, *you can breathe. How long has it been? Three years? Four? That slime ball Jackson almost got us. But we got him, we won. Morris is free now; you can relax. Maybe take a vacation, Boca Grande? Aruba? Maybe spend some time down in the Keys...*

"There it is!" she yelled sitting up straighter interrupting his thoughts. "Did you see it? It was right there!" She pointed to nowhere in particular. He sighed, he was in too good of a mood to be frustrated.

"Yeah, I think I saw it," he mused. He watched as the little girl licked at her cone in excitement. Wind blew at her dress and she squinted her eyes. Kids and their imaginations. Benny smiled.

Another voice spoke up in his head. *Three kids…killed youngest to oldest and you set him free. Morris did it and you know he did and you defended him. Defended him all the way to freedom. You set a monster lose, Benny. Does it feel good? Do you feel like a hot-shot lawyer?*

There was no choice, he argued. He was a state appointed public defender, what was he supposed to do? Let Morris ride the lethal juice all the way to the wheel in the sky without a hint of legal representation? No, absolutely not. That wasn't what he learned in law school, and not the morals his father had pounded into his head all those late nights in the study.

He murdered kids!

Thunder clapped westward signaling another bout of storms. The wind blew harder sending the few groups of people hurrying towards their cars.

"That's it! Right there! Did you see it? I knew it would be back, I told you!"

Out of the corner of his eye, Benny caught a glimpse of something jump out of the water and then back in. He knew it was a fish but didn't have the heart to tell the little girl. He glanced her way and saw part of the ice cream run down her hand and onto her pink dress.

A gust of wind blew the lake's black water onto the landing in front of him, turning the white stone a dark gray. A younger couple who had been trading secret smiles took a step back and looked anxiously at the approaching storm. Another thunderclap, this one accompanied by a crack of lightening. Geese took flight from across the field. The couple walked away hand in hand. Show's over people time to go home, Mother Nature called with yet another roar of thunder, this one so big he felt it in his chest.

What if he kills again? Will you be able to live with yourself? You're an emotional guy Benny…

A white swirl caught his eye just below the surface, interrupting his thoughts.

"Hey-hey did you see that?" he asked turning to the little girl. She wasn't there. The stone ledge was empty.

Did she look familiar? His mind whispered. Her image rose before him, impossibly curly hair with a purple ribbon clasped to the front wearing a pink back pack. Where...how do you know her? Benny looked around but the park was desolate.

Only you and your thoughts now and wasn't this the reason you came out here? To be alone...think things out. "Holy Christ!" Goosebumps prickled his skin and he knew where he had seen her. Addey Lassing. She was the first of the three Morris killed. Jackson had tugged the heart strings of the jurors showing a slide show of each victim. Addy's photo had affected Benny the most and even then, he had continued to defend Morris.

"I could have found another public defender; there are only a million of them! I could have escaped with some sanity," he cried while beating his fist on the marble railing. Was that a tear or a rain drop? He didn't know.

The heavens let loose buckets of rain. It fell in sheets too thick to see the grassy field beyond; only the lake with its white waves lay visible in front of him.

In the distance, an object floated atop the water. He stared, rubbing disbelief from his eyes. It was Addey with her pink dress billowing out around her.

"Addey!" he called.

"Please help me!" Her voice was faint and gurgled.

"I'm coming just stay there!"

Rain stung his eyes and Benny turned away only to face a boy standing inches from him. His hair fell across his eyes and dark purple bruises ran across his neck. *John... he was the second, strangled and drowned...*

"What the fuck," he breathed looking back to the water. Addey was gone. Benny squeezed his eyes shut until his head throbbed. His thoughts danced together and his mind turned into hysterics.

It's the rain, playing a trick on your eyes. The rain...the storm...it's just garbage. But what if it wasn't? What if they're really alive? That would mean Morris is innocent!

"He's innocent! Morris is innocent!" he cried thrusting his fist in the air and opening his eyes. He saw Sarah, the last of the three, standing with John and Addey in front of him. The wind blew but their clothes did not. Even Sarah's long auburn hair lay flat against her back.

"Take that Jackson! You shit sandwich! I knew he didn't do it! Knew it all along!" he said walking closer to the kids. They took a step back in unison. "How did you- where did you- none of that matters!" He laughed wildly. "We have to get you three out of this storm and to the courthouse!" Benny stumbled towards them.

Addey smiled and held out her hand

"I knew he was innocent! All along I knew he was innocent! Wouldn't dad be proud wouldn't..." Addey grasped his hand with unnatural strength, breaking every bone in a wicked crunch that harmonized with the thunder and lightning overhead. John reached out and clasped his shoulder, sending white hot pain searing down his spine. Benny screamed but no one heard. Together, Addey pulled and John pushed forcing Benny to fall hard on his knees. Dreadful fear clenched his heart making it hard to breathe.

"He's innocent though! Please god no!"

The four fell backwards into the water, Addey's grip dragging his limp hand and John's touch burning through his body. Sarah clenched at his leg pulling him deeper. Cold water filled his mouth and lungs. His eyes, wide with horror, watched as the children dragged him further and further down. He screamed but only bubbles escaped. The last thing Benny Huntington saw was the smile on Addey Lassing's dead face as she dragged him into the dark depths.

Luke Chapman *resides in St. Louis, Missouri, home of toasted ravioli's and the Blues. He attends St. Louis Community College as an English major, and is the author of* There's Something in the Water. *When not writing, you can find him at the gym or curled around a good book. You can connect with Luke on Facebook at Luke Chapman, or on Instagram @lj_chap or Twitter @LJ_Chap.*

www.ingramcontent.com/pod-product-compliance
Lightning Source LLC
Chambersburg PA
CBHW020143150626
46552CB00021B/1593